The Twelve Days of Christmas

The Twelve Days of
CHRISTMAS

Illustrated by Don Daily

COURAGE
BOOKS

AN IMPRINT OF RUNNING PRESS
PHILADELPHIA • LONDON

Library of Congress Cataloging-in-Publication Number 00-132365
ISBN-10: 0-7624-2877-5
ISBN-13: 978-0-7624-2877-9

Cover and interior design by Frances J. Soo Ping Chow
Edited by Greg Jones and Danielle McCole

This book may be ordered by mail from the publisher.
But try your bookstore first!

Published by Courage Books, an imprint of
Running Press Book Publishers
2300 Chestnut Street
Philadelphia, Pennsylvania 19103-4371

Visit us on the web!
www.runningpress.com

On the 1st day of Christmas

my true love gave to me

A partridge in a pear tree.

On the 2nd day of Christmas

my true love gave to me

Two turtle doves and a partridge in a pear tree.

On the 3rd day of Christmas

my true love gave to me

Three French hens, two turtle doves, and a partridge

in a pear tree.

On the 4th day of Christmas
my true love gave to me

Four calling birds, three French hens, two turtle
doves, and a partridge in a pear tree.

On the 5th day of Christmas
my true love gave to me

Five golden rings, four calling birds, three
French hens, two turtle doves, and a partridge
in a pear tree.

On the 6th day of Christmas my true love gave to me

Six geese a-laying, five golden rings, four calling birds, three French hens, two turtle doves, and a partridge in a pear tree.

On the 7th day of Christmas
my true love gave to me

Seven swans a-swimming, six geese a-laying, five
golden rings, four calling birds, three French hens,
two turtle doves, and a partridge in a pear tree.

On the 8th day of Christmas
my true love gave to me

Eight maids a-milking, seven swans a-swimming,
six geese a-laying, five golden rings, four calling
birds, three French hens, two turtle doves, and a
partridge in a pear tree.

On the **9th** day of
Christmas my true love gave to me

Nine ladies dancing, eight maids
a-milking, seven swans a-swimming,
six geese a-laying, five golden rings,
four calling birds, three French hens,
two turtle doves, and a partridge
in a pear tree.

On the 10th day of Christmas

my true love gave to me

Ten lords a-leaping, nine ladies dancing, eight maids a-milking, seven swans a-swimming, six geese a-laying, five golden
rings, four calling birds, three French hens, two turtle doves,
and a partridge in a pear tree.

On the 11th day of Christmas
my true love gave to me

Eleven pipers piping, ten lords a-leaping, nine ladies dancing, eight maids a-milking, seven swans a-swimming, six geese a-laying, five golden rings, four calling birds, three French hens, two turtle doves, and a partridge in a pear tree.

On the **12th** day of Christmas

my true love gave to me

Twelve drummers drumming, eleven pipers piping, ten lords
a-leaping, nine ladies dancing, eight maids a-milking, seven
swans a-swimming, six geese a-laying, five golden rings, four
calling birds, three French hens, two turtle doves, and a partridge in a pear tree.